Franklin Has a Sleepover

Franklin

Franklin is a trade mark of Kids Can Press Ltd.

Text copyright © 1996 by P.B. Creations Inc.
Illustrations copyright © 1996 by Brenda Clark Illustrator Inc.
Interior illustrations prepared with the assistance of
Muriel Hughes Wood.

Kids Can Press Ltd.
29 Birch Avenue
Toronto, Ontario, Canada
M4V 1E2

Printed in Hong Kong by Wing King Tong Co. Ltd.

CDN PA 96 0 9 8 7

Canadian Cataloguing in Publication Data

Bourgeois, Paulette
    Franklin has a sleepover

ISBN   1-55074-300-7 (bound)   ISBN   1-55074-302-3 (pbk.)

1. Picture books for children. I. Clark, Brenda. II. Title.

PS8553.085477F73 1996   jC813'.54   C95-932103-9
PZ7.B68Fr 1996

Kids Can Press is a Nelvana company

Franklin Has a Sleepover

Written by Paulette Bourgeois
Illustrated by Brenda Clark

Kids Can Press

FRANKLIN could count by twos and tie his shoes. He could zip zippers and button buttons. He could even sleep alone in his small, dark shell. So Franklin thought he was ready for his first sleepover. He asked his mother if Bear could stay overnight.

"All right," said Franklin's mother. "But where will Bear sleep?"

Franklin's room was small for a turtle *and* a bear.

"We could sleep in the living room," suggested Franklin. "And we could have a campfire outside and ..."

"Wait a minute!" laughed Franklin's mother. "You haven't even asked Bear yet."

Bear did a happy dance after Franklin called.
"May I please go?" he asked.
His parents worried that the two friends would keep each other awake all night.
"We'll sleep," promised Bear.
Then they wondered if he would feel homesick.
"Not me!" said Bear.
So his parents said yes.

Bear called Franklin. "I can come! I can come!" he shouted.

Franklin could hardly wait. Bear wouldn't arrive until after supper, and Franklin had just finished lunch. So he sorted all his toys and picked Bear's favourites. He made sure there was enough to eat. He even tidied his room. Franklin wanted everything to be just right for his first sleepover.

Bear was excited, too. He couldn't decide what to bring and what to leave behind. He filled an enormous bag with toys, books, a pillow, a sleeping bag, a puzzle and a flashlight. He packed slippers, a toothbrush and a snack. He put his bunny on top of the bag. And every hour he asked if it was time to go.

After supper, Franklin sat by the window, waiting for his friend. Finally, Bear and his parents arrived.

"Have a good time," they said. Bear gave them each a great big hug.

"We're camping in the living room," said Franklin.

"Oh, I've never done that before," said Bear.

He laid out his sleeping bag and Franklin made a tent from a tablecloth.

"This is going to be so much fun," giggled Bear.

They played all their favourite games. Before
long it was dark outside.

"How about a campfire?" asked Franklin's father.

"With marshmallows?" Bear licked his lips.

"And hot dogs too," said Franklin's mother.

Franklin's father told Bear and Franklin what
to do. They gathered sticks and twigs at the edge
of the woods and helped to lay the fire. They filled
a bucket with sand and another with water.

"I'll light the fire," said Franklin's mother.

There was a crackle, and sparks jumped into
the air.

"I went to camp," said Franklin's father. "We used to sing while the fire was burning."

He sang in a clear, low voice. By the end of the song, Franklin and Bear had learned all the words. The frogs in the pond were croaking, and the owl in the woods was hooting.

Franklin and Bear toasted marshmallows and roasted hot dogs. Bear had two of everything. Then for a long, long time they sat quietly, watching the stars.

Franklin yawned and Bear rubbed his eyes.

"Time to put out the fire and go inside," said Franklin's father.

When Franklin and Bear were ready for bed,
Franklin's parents gave them both a glass of water
and a good-night hug.

"Sleep tight," they said, turning off the light.

The two friends lay still for a moment. Then
Bear turned on his flashlight.

"Franklin?" he whispered. "I don't feel good."

"Did you eat too much?" asked Franklin.

"No," sniffed Bear. A tear ran down his cheek.

"What's wrong then?"

Bear looked around. "I miss my room."

"Oh," said Franklin. Then he had an idea. "Bring your bed and come with me. We can sleep in my room."

Bear found a cosy spot and snuggled into his sleeping bag. After a moment, he turned on his flashlight again.

"What's wrong now?" Franklin asked.

"My mother always says good night to my bunny," whispered Bear.

So Franklin gave the bunny a hug. "Good night, Bunny. Good night, Bear," he said.

Soon they were fast asleep.

The next morning, Franklin's father made them a special breakfast.

"Did you have a nice sleepover?" asked Franklin's mother.

"It was wonderful," said Bear. "Thank you. Next time, may Franklin come to my house?"

"Of course," Franklin's parents laughed.
Franklin did his own happy dance.
"And, Bear," said Franklin, tapping his shell,
"don't worry about where I will sleep. I always
bring my own cosy bed with me!"

Unicorn or dweeb?

"Listen to me, Jessica Wakefield," Janet said angrily. "It's impossible to be both a Unicorn and a dweeb. You're going to have to choose between SOAR! and us."

"Janet, this isn't fair!" Jessica exclaimed.

"I'm giving you two days to decide," Janet said. "We'll have an emergency meeting on Saturday, and you can announce your decision then. It's up to you. Do you want to be a Unicorn—or a social outcast?"

Jessica jumped up and grabbed her backpack. "I can't believe you're doing this to me, Janet," she cried. "I've always been a loyal Unicorn!"

"Well, now you're a loyal dweeb, too," Ellen said.

"This is ridiculous!" Jessica protested.

"It's SOAR! or the Unicorns," Janet said firmly. "You can't have both. You decide."

Bantam Skylark Books in the SWEET VALLEY TWINS AND FRIENDS series.
Ask your bookseller for the books you have missed.

SWEET VALLEY TWINS
AND FRIENDS

Jessica
the
Nerd

Written by
Jamie Suzanne

Created by
FRANCINE PASCAL

A BANTAM SKYLARK BOOK
NEW YORK · TORONTO · LONDON · SYDNEY · AUCKLAND

... and Sweet Valley Twins and Friends are
trademarks of Francine Pascal

Conceived by Francine Pascal

Produced by Daniel Weiss Associates, Inc.
33 West 17th Street
New York, NY 10011

Cover art by James Mathewuse

Skylark Books is a registered trademark of Bantam Books, a division of
Bantam Doubleday Dell Publishing Group, Inc.
Registered in U.S. Patent and Trademark Office and elsewhere.

ISBN 0-553-15963-1

Published simultaneously in the United States and Canada

Bantam Books are published by Bantam Books, a division of Bantam
Doubleday Dell Publishing Group, Inc. Its trademark, consisting of
the words "Bantam Books" and the portrayal of a rooster, is Registered
in U.S. Patent and Trademark Office and in other countries. Marca
Registrada. Bantam Books, 666 Fifth Avenue, New York, New York
10103.

PRINTED IN THE UNITED STATES OF AMERICA

CWO   0 9 8 7 6 5 4 3 2 1